My Lord You
and Palm Court

James Salter

My Lord You
and Palm Court

PICADOR SHOTS

First published 2006 by Picador
an imprint of Pan Macmillan Ltd
Pan Macmillan, 20 New Wharf Road, London N1 9RR
Basingstoke and Oxford
Associated companies throughout the world
www.panmacmillan.com

ISBN-13: 978-0-330-44580-1
ISBN-10: 0-330-44580-4

1 3 5 7 9 8 6 4 2

A CIP catalogue record for this book is available from
the British Library.

Typeset by Intype Libra Ltd
Printed and bound in Great Britain by
Mackays of Chatham plc, Chatham, Kent

My Lord You

THERE WERE CRUMPLED NAPKINS on the table, wine-glasses still with dark remnant in them, coffee stains, and plates with bits of hardened Brie. Beyond the bluish windows the garden lay motionless beneath the birdsong of summer morning. Daylight had come. It had been a success except for one thing: Brennan.

They had sat around first, drinking in the twilight, and then gone inside. The kitchen had a large round table, fireplace, and shelves with ingredients of every kind. Deems was well known as a cook. So was his somewhat unknowable girlfriend, Irene, who had a mysterious smile though they never cooked together. That night it was Deems's turn. He served caviar, brought out in a white jar such as makeup comes in, to be eaten from small silver spoons.

— The only way, Deems muttered in profile. He seldom looked at anyone. Antique silver spoons, Ardis heard him mistakenly say in his low voice, as if it might not have been noticed.

She was noticing everything, however. Though they had known Deems for a while, she and her husband had never been to the house. In the dining room, when they all went in to dinner, she took in the pictures, books, and shelves of objects includ-ing one of perfect, gleaming shells. It was foreign in a way, like anyone else's house, but half-familiar.

There'd been some mix-up about the seating that Irene tried vainly to adjust amid the conver-sation before the meal began. Outside, darkness had come, deep and green. The men were talking about camps they had gone to as boys in piny Maine and about Soros, the financier. Far more interesting was a comment Ardis heard Irene make, in what context she did not know,

— I think there's such a thing as sleeping with one man too many.

— Did you say "such a thing" or "no such thing"? she heard herself ask.

Irene merely smiled. I must ask her later, Ardis thought. The food was excellent. There was cold soup, duck, and a salad of young vegetables. The coffee had been served and Ardis was distractedly playing with melted wax from the candles when a voice burst out loudly behind her,

— I'm late. Who's this? Are these the beautiful people?

It was a drunken man in a jacket and dirty white trousers with blood on them, which had come from nicking his lip while shaving two hours before. His hair was damp, his face arrogant. It was the face of a Regency duke, intimidating, spoiled. The irrational flickered from him.

— Do you have anything to drink here? What is this, wine? Very sorry I'm late. I've just had seven cognacs and said goodbye to my wife. Deems, you know what that's like. You're my only friend, do you know that? The only one.

— There's some dinner in there, if you like, Deems said, gesturing toward the kitchen.

— No dinner. I've had dinner. I'll just have something to drink. Deems, you're my friend, but I'll tell you something, you'll become my enemy. You know what Oscar Wilde said—my favorite writer, my favorite in all the world. Anyone can choose his friends, but only the wise man can choose his enemies.

He was staring intently at Deems. It was like the grip of a madman, a kind of fury. His mouth had an expression of determination. When he went into the kitchen they could hear him among the bottles. He returned with a dangerous glassful and looked around boldly.

— Where is Beatrice? Deems asked.

— Who?

— Beatrice, your wife.

— Gone, Brennan said.

He searched for a chair.

— To visit her father? Irene asked.

— What makes you think that? Brennan said

6

menacingly. To Ardis's alarm he sat down next to her.

— He's been in the hospital, hasn't he?

— Who knows where he's been, Brennan said darkly. He's a swine. Lucre, gain. He's a slum owner, a criminal. I would hang him myself. In the fashion of Gomez, the dictator, whose daughters are probably wealthy women.

He discovered Ardis and said to her, as if imitating someone, perhaps someone he assumed her to be,

— 'N 'at funny? 'N 'at wonderful?

To her relief he turned away.

— I'm their only hope, he said to Irene. I'm living on their money and it's ruinous, the end of me. He held out his glass and asked mildly, Can I have just a tiny bit of ice? I adore my wife. To Ardis he confided, Do you know how we met? Unimaginable. She was walking by on the beach. I was unprepared. I saw the ventral, then the dorsal, I imagined the rest. Bang! We came together like planets. Endless fornication. Sometimes I just lie silent and observe her. *The black panther lies under his rose-tree*, he recited, *J'ai eu pitié des autres . . .*

He stared at her.

— What is that? she asked tentatively.

— *. . . but that the child walk in peace in her basilica*, he intoned.

— Is it Wilde?

— You can't guess? Pound. The sole genius of the century. No, not the sole. I am another: a drunk, a failure, and a great genius. Who are you? he said. Another little housewife?

She felt the blood leave her face and stood to busy herself clearing the table. His hand was on her arm.

— Don't go. I know who you are, another priceless woman meant to languish. Beautiful figure, he said as she managed to free herself, pretty shoes.

As she carried some plates into the kitchen she could hear him saying,

— Don't go to many of these parties. Not invited.

— Can't imagine why, someone murmured.

8

— But Deems is my friend, my very closest friend.

— Who is he? Ardis asked Irene in the kitchen.

— Oh, he's a poet. He's married to a Venezuelan woman and she runs off. He's not always this bad.

They had quieted him down in the other room. Ardis could see her husband nervously pushing his glasses up on his nose with one finger. Deems, in a polo shirt and with rumpled hair, was trying to guide Brennan toward the back door. Brennan kept stopping to talk. For a moment he would seem reformed.

— I want to tell you something, he said. I went past the school, the one on the street there. There was a poster. The First Annual Miss Fuck Contest. I'm serious. This is a fact.

— No, no, Deems said.

— It's been held, I don't know when. Question is, are they coming to their senses finally or losing them? A tiny bit more, he begged; his glass was empty. His mind doubled back, Seriously, what do you think of that?

In the light of the kitchen he seemed merely dishevelled, like a journalist who has been working hard all night. The unsettling thing was the absence of reason in him, his glare. One nostril was smaller than the other. He was used to being ungovernable. Ardis hoped he would not notice her again. His forehead had two gleaming places, like nascent horns. Were men drawn to you when they knew they were frightening you?

She could feel his eyes. There was silence. She could feel him standing there like a menacing beggar.

— What are you, another bourgeois? he said to her. I know I've been drinking. Come and have dinner, he said. I've ordered something wonderful for us. Vichyssoise. Lobster. S. G. Always on the menu like that, *selon grosseur*.

He was talking in an easy way, as if they were in the casino together, chips piled high before them, as if it were a shrewd discussion of what to bet on and her breasts in the dark T-shirt were a thing of indifference to him. He calmly reached out and touched one.

— I have money, he said. His hand remained where it was, cupping her. She was too stunned to move. Do you want me to do more of that?

— No, she managed to say.

His hand slipped down to her hip. Deems had taken an arm and was drawing him away.

— Ssh, Brennan whispered to her, don't say anything. The two of us. Like an oar going into the water, gliding.

— We have to go, Deems insisted.

— What are you doing? Is this another of your ruses? Brennan cried. Deems, I shall end up destroying you yet!

As he was herded to the door, he continued. Deems was the only man he didn't loathe, he said. He wanted them all to come to his house, he had everything. He had a phonograph, whisky! He had a gold watch!

At last he was outside. He walked unsteadily across the finely cut grass and got into his car, the side of which was dented in. He backed away in great lurches.

— He's headed for Cato's, Deems guessed. I ought to call and warn them.

— They won't serve him. He owes them money, Irene said.

— Who told you that?

— The bartender. Are you all right? she asked Ardis.

— Yes. Is he actually married?

— He's been married three or four times, Deems said.

Later they started dancing, some of the women together. Irene pulled Deems onto the floor. He came unresisting. He danced quite well. She was moving her arms sinuously and singing.

— Very nice, he said. Have you ever entertained?

She smiled at him.

— I do my best, she said.

At the end she put her hand on Ardis's arm and said again,

— I'm so embarrassed at what happened.

— It was nothing. I'm all right.

— I should have taken him and thrown him

out, her husband said on the way home. Ezra Pound. Do you know about Ezra Pound?

— No.

— He was a traitor. He broadcast for the enemy during the war. They should have shot him.

— What happened to him?

— They gave him a poetry prize.

They were going down a long empty stretch where on a corner, half hidden in trees, a small house stood, the gypsy house, Ardis thought of it as, a simple house with a water pump in the yard and occasionally in the daytime a girl in blue shorts, very brief, and high heels, hanging clothes on a line. Tonight there was a light on in the window. One light near the sea. She was driving with Warren and he was talking.

— The best thing is to just forget about tonight.

— Yes, she said. It was nothing.

Brennan went through a fence on Hull Lane and up on to somebody's lawn at about two that morning. He had missed the curve where the road bent left, probably because his headlights weren't on, the police thought.

She took the book and went over to a window that looked out on the garden behind the library. She read a bit of one thing or another and came to a poem some lines of which had been underlined, with pencilled notes in the margin. It was "The River-Merchant's Wife"; she had never heard of it. Outside, the summer burned, white as chalk.

At fourteen I married My Lord you, she read.
I never laughed, being bashful . . .

There were three old men, one of them almost blind, it appeared, reading newspapers in the cold room. The thick glasses of the nearly blind man cast white moons onto his cheeks.

The leaves fall early this autumn, in wind.
The paired butterflies are already yellow with
　　August
Over the grass in the West garden;
They hurt me. I grow older.

She had read poems and perhaps marked them like this, but that was in school. Of the things she had been taught she remembered only a few. There had been one My Lord though she did not marry him. She'd been twenty-one, her first year in the city. She remembered the building of dark brown brick on Fifty-eighth Street, the afternoons with their slitted light, her clothes in a chair or fallen to the floor, and the damp, mindless repetition, to it, or him, or who knew what: oh, God, oh, God, oh, God. The traffic outside so faint, so far away . . .

She'd called him several times over the years, believing that love never died, dreaming foolishly of seeing him again, of his returning, in the way of old songs. To hurry, to almost run down the noon-time street again, the sound of her heels on the side-walk. To see the door of the apartment open . . .

If you are coming down the narrows of the
  river Kiang,
Please let me know beforehand,
And I will come out to meet you.
  As far as Chô-fu-Sa

There she sat by the window with her young face that had a weariness in it, a slight distaste for things, even, one might imagine for oneself. After a while she went to the desk.

— Do you happen to have anything by Michael Brennan? she asked.

— Michael Brennan, the woman said. We've had them, but he takes them away because unworthy people read them, he says. I don't think there're any now. Perhaps when he comes back from the city.

— He lives in the city?

— He lives just down the road. We had all of his books at one time. Do you know him?

She would have liked to ask more but she shook her head.

— No, she said. I've just heard the name.

— He's a poet, the woman said.

On the beach she sat by herself. There was almost no one. In her bathing suit she lay back with the sun on her face and knees. It was hot and the sea calm. She preferred to lie up by the dunes with the waves bursting, to listen while they crashed like the final chords of a symphony except they went on and on. There was nothing as fine as that.

She came out of the ocean and dried herself like the gypsy girl, ankles caked with sand. She could feel the sun burnishing her shoulders. Hair wet, deep in the emptiness of days, she walked her bicycle up to the road, the dirt velvety beneath her feet.

She did not go home the usual way. There was little traffic. The noon was bottle-green, large houses among the trees and wide farmland, like a memory, behind.

She knew the house and saw it far off, her heart beating strangely. When she stopped, it was casually, with the bike tilting to one side and she half-seated on it as if taking a rest. How beautiful a lone woman is, in a white summer shirt and bare legs. Pretending to adjust the bicycle's chain she looked at the house, its tall windows, water stains high on the roof. There was a gardener's shed, abandoned, saplings growing in the path that led

17

to it. The long driveway, the sea porch, everything was empty.

Walking slowly, aware of how brazen she was, she went toward the house. Her urge was to look in the windows, no more than that. Still, despite the silence, the complete stillness, that was forbidden.

She walked farther. Suddenly someone rose from the side porch. She was unable to utter a sound or move.

It was a dog, a huge dog higher than her waist, coming toward her, yellow-eyed. She had always been afraid of dogs, the Alsatian that had unexpectedly turned on her college roommate and torn off a piece of her scalp. The size of this one, its lowered head and slow, deliberate stride.

Do not show fear, she knew that. Carefully she moved the bicycle so that it was between them. The dog stopped a few feet away, its eyes directly on her, the sun along its back. She did not know what to expect, a sudden short rush.

— Good boy, she said. It was all she could think of. Good boy.

Moving cautiously, she began wheeling the

bicycle toward the road, turning her head away slightly so as to appear unworried. Her legs felt naked, the bare calves. They would be ripped open as if by a scythe. The dog was following her, its shoulders moving smoothly, like a kind of machine. Somehow finding the courage, she tried to ride. The front wheel wavered. The dog, high as the handlebars, came nearer.

— No, she cried. No!

After a moment or two, obediently, he slowed or veered off. He was gone.

She rode as if freed, as if flying through blocks of sunlight and high, solemn tunnels of trees. And then she saw him again. He was following—not exactly following, since he was some distance ahead. He seemed to float along in the fields, which were burning in the midday sun, on fire. She turned onto her own road. There he came. He fell in behind her. She could hear the clatter of his nails like falling stones. She looked back. He was trotting awkwardly, like a big man running in the rain. A line of spittle trailed from his jaw. When she reached her house he had disappeared.

That night in a cotton robe she was preparing for bed, cleaning her face, the bathroom door ajar. She brushed her hair with many rapid strokes.

— Tired? her husband asked as she emerged.

It was his way of introducing the subject.

— No, she said.

So there they were in the summer night with the far-off sound of the sea. Among the things her husband admired that Ardis possessed was extraordinary skin, luminous and smooth, a skin so pure that to touch it would make one tremble.

— Wait, she whispered, —not so fast.

Afterward he lay back without a word, already falling into deepest sleep, much too soon. She touched his shoulder. She heard something outside the window.

— Did you hear that?

— No, what? he said drowsily.

She waited. There was nothing. It had seemed faint, like a sigh.

The next morning she said,

— Oh! There, just beneath the trees, the dog lay. She could see his ears—they were small ears dashed with white.

— What is it? her husband asked.

— Nothing, she said. A dog. It followed me yesterday.

— From where? he said, coming to see.

— Down the road. I think it might be that man's. Brennan's.

— Brennan?

— I passed his house, she said, and afterward it was following me.

— What were you doing at Brennan's?

— Nothing. I was passing. He's not even there.

— What do you mean, he's not there?

— I don't know. Somebody said that.

He went to the door and opened it. The dog— it was a deerhound—had been lying with its forelegs stretched out in front like a sphinx, its haunches round and high. Awkwardly it rose and after a moment moved, reluctantly it seemed, wandering slowly across the fields, never looking back.

In the evening they went to a party on Mecox Road. Far out toward Montauk, winds were sweeping the coast. The waves exploded in clouds of spray. Ardis was talking to a woman not much older than herself, whose husband had just died of a brain tumor at the age of forty. He had diagnosed it himself, the woman said. He'd been sitting in a theater when he suddenly realized he couldn't see the wall just to his right. At the funeral, she said, there had been two women she did not recognize and who did not come to the reception afterward.

— Of course, he was a surgeon, she said, and they're drawn to surgeons like flies. But I never suspected. I suppose I'm the world's greatest fool.

The trees streamed past in the dark as they drove home. Their house rose in the brilliant headlights. She thought she had caught sight of something and found herself hoping her husband had not. She was nervous as they walked across the grass. The stars were numberless. They would open the door and go inside, where all was familiar, even serene.

After a while they would prepare for bed while the wind seized the corners of the house and the dark leaves thrashed each other. They would turn out the lights. All that was outside would be left in wildness, in the glory of the wind.

It was true. He was there. He was lying on his side, his whitish coat ruffled. In the morning light she approached slowly. When he raised his head his eyes were hazel and gold.

He was not that young, she saw, but his power was that he was unbowed. She spoke in a natural voice.

— Come, she said.

She took a few steps. At first he did not move. She glanced back again. He was following.

It was still early. As they reached the road a car passed, drab and sun-faded. A girl was in the back seat, head fallen wearily, being driven home, Ardis thought, after the exhausting night. She felt an inexplicable envy.

It was warm but the true heat had not risen.

Several times she waited while he drank from puddles at the edge of the road, standing in them as he did, his large, wet toenails gleaming like ivory.

Suddenly from a porch rushed another dog, barking fiercely. The great hound turned, teeth bared. She held her breath, afraid of the sight of one of them limp and bleeding, but violent as it sounded they kept a distance between them. After a few snaps it was over. He came along less steadily, strands of wet hair near his mouth.

At the house he went to the porch and stood waiting. It was plain he wanted to go inside. He had returned. He must be starving, she thought. She looked around to see if there was anyone in sight. A chair she had not noticed before was out on the grass, but the house was as still as ever, not even the curtains breathing. With a hand that seemed not even hers she tried the door. It was unlocked.

The hallway was dim. Beyond it was a living room in disorder, couch cushions rumpled, glasses on the tables, papers, shoes. In the dining room there were piles of books. It was the house of an artist, abundance, disregard.

There was a large desk in the bedroom, in the middle of which, among paper clips and letters, a space had been cleared. Here were sheets of paper written in an almost illegible hand, incomplete lines and words that omitted certain vowels. *Deth of fathr*, she read, then indecipherable things and something that seemed to be *carrges sent empty*, and at the bottom, set apart, two words, *anew, anew*. In a different hand was the page of a letter, *I deeply love you. I admire you. I love you and admire you.* She could not read anymore. She was too uneasy. There were things she did not want to know. In a hammered silver frame was the photograph of a woman, face darkened by shadow, leaning against a wall, the unseen white of a villa somewhere behind. Through the slatted blinds one could hear the soft clack of palm fronds, the birds high above, in the villa where he had found her, where her youth had been bold as a declaration of war. No, that was not it. He had met her on a beach, they had gone to the villa. What is powerful is a glimpse of a truer life. She read the slanting inscription in Spanish, *Tus besos me destierran*. She put the picture down. A photograph was sacrosanct, you were excluded from it, always. So that was the wife. *Tus besos*, your kisses.

She wandered, nearly dreaming, into a large bathroom that looked out on the garden. As she entered, her heart almost stopped—she caught sight of somebody in the mirror. It took a second before she realized it was herself and, as she looked more closely, a not wholly recognizable, even an illicit self, in soft, grainy light. She understood suddenly, she accepted the fate that meant she was to be found here, that Brennan would be returning and discover her, having stopped for the mail or bread. Out of nowhere she would hear the paralyzing sound of footsteps or a car. Still, she continued to look at herself. She was in the house of the poet, the demon. She had entered forbidden rooms. *Tus besos* . . . the words had not died. At that moment the dog came to the door, stood there, and then fell to the floor, his knowing eyes on her, like an intimate friend. She turned to him. All she had never done seemed at hand.

Deliberately, without thinking, she began to remove her clothes. She went no further than the waist. She was dazzled by what she was doing. There in the silence with the sunlight outside she stood slender and half-naked, the missing image of herself, of all women. The dog's eyes were raised to her as if in reverence. He was unbetraying, a companion like no other. She remembered certain figures ahead of her at school. Kit Vining, Nan Boudreau. Legendary faces and reputations. She had longed to be like them but never seemed to have the chance. She leaned forward to stroke the beautiful head.

— You're a big fellow. The words seemed authentic, more authentic than anything she had said for a long time. A very big fellow.

His long tail stirred and with faint sound brushed the floor. She kneeled and stroked his head again and again.

There was the crackling of gravel beneath the tires of a car. It brought her abruptly to her senses. Hurriedly, almost in panic, she threw on her clothes and made her way to the kitchen. She would run along the porch if necessary and then from tree to tree.

She opened the door and listened. Nothing. As she was going quickly down the back steps, by the side of the house she saw her husband. Thank God, she thought helplessly.

They approached each other slowly. He glanced at the house.

— I brought the car. Is anyone here? There was a moment's pause.

— No, no one. She felt her face stiffen, as if she were telling a lie.

— What were you doing? he asked.

— I was in the kitchen, she said. I was trying to find something to feed him.

— Did you find it?

— Yes. No, she said.

He stood looking at her and finally said,

— Let's go.

As they backed out, she caught sight of the dog just lying down in the shade, sprawled, disconsolate. She felt the nakedness beneath her clothes, the satisfaction. They turned onto the road.

— Somebody's got to feed him, she said as they drove. She was looking out at the houses and fields. Warren said nothing. He was driving faster. She turned back to look. For a moment she thought she saw him following, far behind.

Late that day she went shopping and came home about five. The wind, which had arisen anew, blew the door shut with a bang.

— Warren?

— Did you see him? her husband said.

— Yes.

He had come back. He was out there where the land went up slightly.

— I'm going to call the animal shelter, she said.

— They won't do anything. He's not a stray.

— I can't stand it. I'm calling someone, she said.

— Why don't you call the police? Maybe they'll shoot him.

— Why don't you do it? she said coldly. Borrow someone's gun. He's driving me crazy.

It remained light until past nine, and in the last of it, with the clouds a deeper blue than the sky, she went out quietly, far across the grass. Her husband watched from the window. She was carrying a white bowl.

She could see him very clearly, the gray of his muzzle there in the muted grass and when she was close the clear, tan eyes. In an almost ceremonial way she knelt down. The wind was blowing her hair. She seemed almost a mad person there in the fading light.

— Here. Drink something, she said.

His gaze, somehow reproachful, drifted away. He was like a fugitive sleeping on his coat. His eyes were nearly closed.

My life has meant nothing, she thought. She wanted above all else not to confess that.

They ate dinner in silence. Her husband did not look at her. Her face annoyed him, he did not know why. She could be good-looking but there were times when she was not. Her face was like a series of photographs, some of which ought to have been thrown away. Tonight it was like that.

— The sea broke through into Sag Pond today, she said dully.

— Did it?

— They thought some little girl had drowned. The fire trucks were there. It turned out she had just strayed off. After a pause, We have to do something, she said.

— Whatever happens is going to happen, he told her.

— This is different, she said. She suddenly left the room. She felt close to tears.

Her husband's business was essentially one of giving advice. He had a life that served other lives, helped them come to agreements, end marriages, defend themselves against former friends. He was accomplished at it. Its language and techniques were part of him. He lived amid disturbance and self-interest but always protected from it. In his files were letters, memorandums, secrets of careers. One thing he had seen: how near men could be to disaster no matter how secure they seemed. He had seen events turn, one ruinous thing following another. It could happen without warning. Sometimes they were able to save themselves, but there was a point at which they could not. He sometimes wondered about himself—when the blow came and the beams began to give and come apart, what would happen? She was calling Brennan's house again. There was never an answer.

During the night the wind blew itself out. In the morning at first light, Warren could feel the stillness. He lay in bed without moving. His wife's back was turned toward him. He could feel her denial.

He rose and went to the window. The dog was still there, he could see its shape. He knew little of animals and nothing of nature but he could tell what had happened. It was lying in a different way.

— What is it? she asked. She had come up beside him. It seemed she stood there for a long time. He's dead.

She started for the door. He held her by the arm.

— Let me go, she said.

— Ardis . . .

She began to weep,

— Let me go.

— Leave him alone! he called after her. Let him be!

She ran quickly across the grass in her night-gown. The ground was wet. As she came closer she paused to calm herself, to find courage. She regretted only one thing—she had not said good-bye.

She took a step or two forward. She could sense the heavy, limp weight of him, a weight that would disperse, become something else, the sinews fading, the bones becoming light. She longed to do what she had never done, embrace him. At that moment he raised his head.

— Warren! she cried, turning toward the house. Warren!

As if the shouts distressed him, the dog was rising to his feet. He moved wearily off. Hands pressed to her mouth, she stared at the place where he had been, where the grass was flattened slightly. All night again. Again all night. When she looked, he was some distance off.

She ran after him. Warren could see her. She seemed free. She seemed like another woman, a younger woman, the kind one saw in the dusty fields by the sea, in a bikini, stealing potatoes in bare feet.

She did not see him again. She went many times past the house, occasionally seeing Brennan's car there, but never a sign of the dog, or along the road or off in the fields.

One night in Cato's at the end of August, she saw Brennan himself at the bar. His arm was in a sling, from what sort of accident she could not guess. He was talking intently to the bartender, the same fierce eloquence, and though the restaurant was crowded, the stools next to him were empty. He was alone. The dog was not outside, nor in his car, nor part of his life anymore—gone, lost, living elsewhere, his name perhaps to be written in a line someday though most probably he was forgotten, but not by her.

Palm Court

Late one afternoon, near the close, his assistant, Kenny, palm over the mouthpiece, said there was someone named Noreen on the phone.

— You know her, she says.

— Noreen? I'll take it, Arthur said. Just a minute.

He got up and closed the door to his cubicle. He was still visible through the glass as he sat and turned toward the window, distancing himself from all that was going on, the dozens of customers' men, some of them women, which once would have been unthinkable, looking at their screens and talking on the phone. His heart was tripping faster when he spoke.

— Hello?

— Arthur?

The one word and a kind of shiver went through him, a frightened happiness, as when your name is called by the teacher.

— It's Noreen, she said.

— Noreen. How are you? God, it's been a long time. Where are you?

— I'm here. I'm living back here now, she said.

— No kidding. What happened?

— We broke up.

— That's too bad, he said. I'm sorry to hear that.

He always seemed completely sincere, even in the most ordinary comments.

— It was a mistake, she said. I never should have done it. I should have known.

The floor around the desk was strewn with paper, reports, annual statements with their many numbers. That was not his strength. He liked to talk to people, he could talk and tell stories all day. And he was known to be honest. He had taken as models the old-timers, men long gone such as Henry Braver, Patsy Millinger's father, who'd been a partner and had started before the war. Onassis had been one of his clients. Braver had an international reputation as well as a nose for the real thing. Arthur didn't have the nose, but he could talk and listen. There were all kinds of ways of making money in this business. His way was finding one or two big winners to go down and double on. And he talked to his clients every day.

— Mark, how are you, tootsula? You ought to be here. The numbers came in on Micronics. They're all crying. We were so smart not to get involved in that. Sweetheart, you want to know something? There are some very smart guys here who've taken a bath. He lowered his voice. Morris, for one.

— Morris? They should give him an injection. Put him to sleep.

— He was a little too smart this time. Living through the Depression didn't help this time.

Morris had a desk near the copy machine, a courtesy desk. He had been a partner, but after he retired there was nothing to do—he hated Florida and didn't play golf—and so he came back to the firm and traded for himself. His age alone set him apart. He was a relic with perfect, false teeth and lived in some amberoid world with an aged wife. They all joked about him. The years had left him, as if marooned, alone at his desk and in an apartment on Park Avenue no one had ever been to.

Morris had lost a lot on Micronics. It was impossible to say how much. He kept his own shaky figures, but Arthur had gotten it out of Marie, the sexless woman who cleared trades.

— A hundred thousand, she said. Don't say anything.

— Don't worry, darling, Arthur told her.

Arthur knew everything and was on the phone all day. It was one unending conversation: gossip, affection, news. He looked like Punch, with a curved nose, up-pointing chin, and innocent smile. He was filled with happiness, but the kind that knew its limits. He had been at Frackman, Wells from the time there were seven employees, and now there were nearly two hundred with three floors in the building. He himself had become rich, beyond anything he could have imagined,

although his life had not changed and he still had
the same apartment in London Terrace. He was
living there the night he first met Noreen in
Goldie's. She did something few girls had ever
done with him, she laughed and sat close. From
the first moment there was openness between
them. Noreen. The piano rippling away, the old
songs, the noise.

— I'm divorced, she said. How about you?

— Me? The same, he said.

The street below was filled with hurrying people, cars. The sound of it was faint.

— Really? she said.

It had been years since he had talked to her.
There was a time they had been inseparable. They
were at Goldie's every night or at Clarke's, where
he also went regularly. They always gave him a
good table, in the middle section with the side
door or in back with the crowd and the unchang-
ing menu written neatly in chalk. Sometimes they
stood in front at the long, scarred bar with the
sign that said under no circumstances would women
be served there. The manager, the bartenders,

waiters, everybody knew him. Clarke's was his real home; he merely went elsewhere to sleep. He drank very little despite his appearance, but he always paid for drinks and stayed at the bar for hours, occasionally taking a few steps to the men's room, a pavilion of its own, long and old-fashioned, where you urinated like a grand duke on blocks of ice. To Clarke's came advertising men, models, men like himself, and off-duty cops late at night. He showed Noreen how to recognize them, black shoes and white socks. Noreen loved it. She was a favorite there, with her looks and wonderful laugh. The waiters called her by her first name.

Noreen was dark blond, though her mother was Greek, she said. There were a lot of blonds in the north of Greece where her family came from. The ranks of the Roman legions had become filled with Germanic tribesmen as time passed, and when Rome fell some of the scattered legions settled in the mountains of Greece; at least that was the way she had heard it.

— So I'm Greek but I'm German, too, she told Arthur.

— God, I hope not, he said. I couldn't go with a German.

— What do you mean?

— Be seen with.

— Arthur, she explained, you have to accept the way things are, what I am and what you are and why it's so good.

There were things she wanted to tell him but didn't, things he wouldn't like to hear, or so she felt. About being a young girl and the night at the St. George Hotel when she was nineteen and went upstairs with a guy she thought was really nice. They went to his boss's suite. The boss was away and they were drinking his twelve-year-old scotch, and the next thing she knew she was lying face-down on the bed with her hands tied behind her. That was in a different world than Arthur's. His was decent, forgiving, warm.

They went together for nearly three years, the best years. They saw one another almost every night. She knew all about his work. He could make it seem so interesting, the avid individuals, the partners, Buddy Frackman, Warren Sender. And Morris; she had actually seen Morris once on the elevator.

— You're looking very well, she told him nervily.

— You, too, he said, smiling.

He didn't know who she was, but a few moments later he leaned toward her and silently formed the words,

— Eighty-seven.

— Really?

— Yes, he said proudly.

— I'd never guess.

She knew how, one day coming back from lunch, Arthur and Buddy had seen Morris lying

in the street, his white shirt covered with blood. He had accidentally fallen, and there were two or three people trying to help him up.

— Don't look. Keep going, Arthur had said.

— He's lucky, having friends like you, Noreen said.

She worked at Grey Advertising, which made it

so convenient to meet. Seeing her always filled him with pleasure, even when it became completely familiar. She was twenty-five and filled with life. That summer he saw her in a bathing suit, a bikini. She was stunning, with a kind of glow to her skin. She had a young girl's unselfconscious belly and ran into the waves. He went in more cautiously, as befitted a man who had been a typist in the army and salesman for a dress manufacturer before coming to what he called Wall Street, where he had always dreamed of being and would have worked for nothing.

The waves, the ocean, the white blinding sand. It was at Westhampton, where they went for the weekend. On the train every seat was taken. Young men in T-shirts and with manly chests were joking in the aisles. Noreen sat beside him, the happiness coming off her like heat. She had a small gold cross, the size of a dime, on a thin gold necklace lying on her shirt. He hadn't noticed it before. He was about to say something when the train began bucking and slowed to a stop.

— What is it? What's happened?

They were not in a station but alongside a low embankment, amid weedy-looking growth. After a while the word came back, they had hit a bicyclist.

— Where? How? Arthur said. We're in a forest.

No one knew much more. People were speculating, should they get off and try to find a taxi; where were they, anyhow? There were guesses. A few individuals did get off and were walking by the side of the train.

— God, I knew something like this would happen, Arthur said.

— Something like this? Noreen said. How could there be something like this?

— When we hit the cow, a man sitting across from them offered.

— The cow? We also hit a cow? Arthur exclaimed.

— A couple of weeks ago, the man explained.

That night Noreen showed him how to eat a lobster.

— My mother would die if she knew this, Arthur said.

— How will she know?

— She'd disown me.

— You start with the claws, Noreen said.

She had tucked the napkin into his collar. They drank some Italian wine.

Westhampton, her tanned legs and pale heels. The feeling she gave him of being younger, even, God help him, debonair. He was playful. On the beach he wore a coconut hat. He had fallen in love, deeply, and without knowing it. He hadn't realized he had been living a shallow life. He only knew that he was happy, happier than he had ever been, in her company. This warmhearted girl with her legs, her fragrance, and perfect little ears that were tuned to him. And she took some kind of pleasure in him! They were guests of the Senders and he slept in a separate room in the basement while she was upstairs, but they were under the same roof and he would see her in the morning.

— When are you going to marry her? everyone asked.

— She wouldn't have me, he equivocated.

Then, offhandedly, she admitted meeting

someone else. It was sort of a joke, Bobby Piro. He was stocky, he lived with his mother, had never married.

— He has black, shiny hair, Arthur guessed as if good-naturedly.

He had to treat it lightly, and Noreen did the same. She would make fun of Bobby when talking about him, his brothers, Dennis and Paul, his wanting to go to Vegas, his mother making chicken Vesuvio, Sinatra's favorite, for her.

— Chicken Vesuvio, Arthur said.

— It was pretty good.

— So you met his mother.

— I'm too skinny, she said.

— She sounds like my mother. Are you sure she's Italian?

She liked Bobby, at least a little, he could see. Still it was difficult to think of him as being really significant. He was someone to talk about. He wanted her to go away on a weekend with him.

— To the Euripides, Arthur said, his stomach suddenly turning over.

— Not that good.

The Euripides Hotel that didn't exist, but that they always joked about because he didn't know who Euripides was.

— Don't let him take you to the Euripides, he said.

— I couldn't do that. It's a Greek place, she said. For us Greeks.

Then, late one night in October, his doorbell rang.

— Who is it? Arthur said.

— It's me.

He opened the door. She stood in the doorway with a smile that he saw had hesitation in it.

— Can I come in?

— Sure, tootsula. Of course. Come in. What's happened, is something wrong?

— There's nothing wrong, really. I just thought I would . . . come by.

The room was clean but somehow barren. He never sat in it and as much as read a book. He lived in the bedroom like a salesman. The curtains hadn't been washed in a long time.

— Here, sit down, he said.

She was walking a bit carefully. She had been drinking, he could see. She felt her way around a chair and sat.

— You want something? Coffee? I'll make some coffee.

She was looking around her.

— You know, I've never been here. This is the first time.

— It's not much of a place. I guess I could find something better.

— Is that the bedroom?

— Yes, he said, but her gaze had drifted from it.

— I just wanted to talk.

— Sure. About what?

He knew, or was afraid he did.

— We've known each other a long time. What has it been, three years?

He felt nervous. The aimless way it was going. He didn't want to disappoint her. On the other hand, he was not sure what it was she wanted. Him? Now?

— You're pretty smart, she said.

— Me? Oh, God, no.

— You understand people. Can you really make some coffee? I think I'd like a cup.

While he busied himself, she sat quietly. He glanced briefly and saw her staring toward the window, beyond which were the lights of apartments in other buildings and the black, starless sky.

— So, she said, holding the coffee, give me some advice. Bobby wants to get married.

Arthur was silent.

— He wants to marry me. The reason I was never serious about him, I was always making fun of him, his being so Italian, his big smile, the reason was that he was involved all that time with some Danish girl. Ode is her name.

— I figured something like that.

— What did you figure?

— Ah, I could see something wasn't right.

— I never met her. I imagined her as being pretty and having this great accent. You know how you torture yourself.

— Ah, Noreen, he said. There's nobody nicer than you.

51

— Anyway, yesterday he told me he'd broken up with her. It was all over. He did it because of me. He realized it was me he loved, and he wanted to marry me.

— Well, that's . . .

Arthur didn't know what to say; his thoughts were skipping wildly, like scraps of paper in a wind. There is that fearful moment in the ceremony when it is asked if there is anyone who knows why these two should not be wed. This was that moment.

— What did you tell him?

— I haven't told him.

A gulf was opening between them somehow. It was happening as they sat there.

— Do you have any feeling about it? she asked.

— Yes, I mean, I'd like to think about it. It's kind of a surprise.

— It was to me, too.

She hadn't touched the coffee.

— You know, I could sit here for a long time, she said. It's as comfortable as I'll ever feel anywhere. That's what's making me wonder. About what to tell him.

— I'm a little afraid, he said. I can't explain it.

— Of course you are. Her voice had such understanding. Really. I know.

— Your coffee's going to get cold, he said.

— Anyway, I just wanted to see your apartment, she said. Her voice suddenly sounded funny. She seemed not to want to go on.

He realized then, as she sat there, a woman in his apartment at night, a woman he knew he loved, that she was really giving him one last chance. He knew he should take it.

— Ah, Noreen, he said.

After that night, she vanished. Not suddenly, but it did not take long. She married Bobby. It was as simple as a death, but it lasted longer. It seemed it would never go away. She lingered in his thoughts. Did he exist in hers? he often wondered. Did she still feel, even if only a little, the way he felt? The years seemed to have no effect on it. She was in New Jersey somewhere, in some place he

could not picture. Probably there was a family.
Did she ever think of him? Ah, Noreen.

She had not changed. He could tell it from her
voice, speaking, as always, to him alone.

— You probably have kids, he said as if
casually.

— He didn't want them. Just one of the prob-
lems. Well, all that's *acqua passata*, as he liked to
say. You didn't know I got divorced?

— No.

— I more or less kept in touch with Marie up
until she retired. She told me how you were doing.
You're a big wheel now.

— Not really.

— I knew you would be. It would be nice to see
you again. How long has it been?

— Gee, a long time.

— You ever go out to Westhampton?

— No, not for years.

— Goldie's?

— He closed.

— I guess I knew that. Those were wonderful days.

It was the same, the ease of talking to her. He saw her great, winning smile, the well-being of it, her carefree walk.

— I'd love to see you, she said again.

They agreed to meet at the Plaza. She was going to be near there the next day.

He began walking up Fifth a little before five. He felt uncertain but tenderhearted, in the hands of a wondrous fate. The hotel stood before him, immense and vaguely white. He walked up the broad steps. There was a kind of foyer with a large table and flowers, the sound of people talking. As if, like an animal, he could detect the slightest noise, he seemed to make out the clink of cups and spoons.

There were flower boxes with pink flowers, the tall columns with their gilded tops, and in the Palm Court itself, which was crowded, through a glass panel he saw her sitting in a chair. For a moment he was not sure it was her. He moved away. Had she seen him?

He could not go in. He turned instead and went down the corridor to the men's room. An old man in black pants and a striped vest, the attendant, offered a towel as Arthur looked at himself in the long mirror to see if he had changed that much, too. He saw a man of fifty-five with the same Coney Island face he had always seen, half comic, kind. No worse than that. He gave the attendant a dollar and walked into the Palm Court, where, amid the chattering tables, the mock candelabra, and illuminated ceiling, Noreen was waiting. He was wearing his familiar dog's smile.

— Arthur, God, you look exactly the same. You haven't changed a bit, she said enthusiastically. I wish I could say that.

It was hard to believe. She was twenty years older; she had gained weight, even her face showed it. She had been the most beautiful girl.

— You look great, he said. I'd recognize you anywhere.

— Life's been good to you, she said.

— Well, I can't complain.

— I guess I can't either. What happened to everybody?

— What do you mean?

— Morris?

— He died. Five or six years ago.

— That's too bad.

— They gave him a big dinner before that. He was all smiles.

— You know, I've wanted to talk to you so much. I wanted to call you, but I was involved in all this tedious divorce stuff. Anyway, I'm finally free. I should have taken your advice.

— What was that?

— Not to marry him, she said.

— I said that?

— No, but I could see you didn't like him.

— I was jealous of him.

— Truly?

— Sure. I mean, let's face it.

She smiled at him.

— Isn't it funny, she said, five minutes with you and it's as if none of it ever happened.

Her clothes, he noticed, even her clothes were hiding who she had been.

— Love never dies, he said.

— Do you mean that?

— You know that.

— Listen, can you have dinner?

— Ah, sweetheart, he said, I'd love to, but I can't. I don't know if you knew this, but I'm engaged.

— Well, congratulations, she said. I didn't know.

He had no idea what had made him say it. It was a word he had never used before in his life.

— That's wonderful, she said straightforwardly, smiling at him with such understanding that he was sure she had seen through him, but he could not imagine them walking into Clarke's, like an old couple, a couple from time past.

— I figured it's time to settle down, he said.

— Of course.

She was not looking at him. She was studying her hands. Then she smiled again. She was forgiving him, he felt. That was it. She always understood.

They talked on, but not about much.

He left through the same foyer with its worn mosaic tile and people coming in. It was still light outside, the pure full light before evening, the sun in a thousand windows facing the park. Walking along the street in their heels, alone or together, were girls such as Noreen had been, many of them. They were not really going to meet for lunch sometime. He thought of the love that had filled the great central chamber of his life and how he would not meet anyone like that again. He did not know what came over him, but on the street he broke into tears.

PICADOR SHOTS

SHALOM AUSLANDER
'Holocaust Tips for Kids' and 'Smite the Heathens,
Charlie Brown' from *Beware of God*

CRAIG DAVIDSON
'A Mean Utility' and 'Life in the Flesh' from *Rust and Bone*

BRET EASTON ELLIS
'Water from the Sun' and 'Discovering Japan'
from *The Informers*

NELL FREUDENBERGER
'Lucky Girls' from *Lucky Girls*

ALEKSANDAR HEMON
'Exchange of Pleasant Words' and 'A Coin'
from *The Question of Bruno*

JACKIE KAY
'Sonata' from *Wish I Was Here*

MATTHEW KNEALE
'Powder' from *Small Crimes in An Age of Abundance*

CLAIRE MESSUD
'The Professor's History'

JAMES SALTER
'My Lord You' and 'Palm Court' from *Last Night*

COLM TÓIBÍN
'The Use of Reason' from *Mothers and Sons*

NIALL WILLIAMS
unpublished new story – 'The Unrequited'

TIM WINTON
'Small Mercies' from *The Turning*

All collections are available in Picador.